P9-DGM-406

Fluttery Butterflies

By Tennant Redbank
Illustrated by Sonja Lamut

Grosset & Dunlap • New York

ISBN 0-448-41838-X   D E F G H I J

Five shimmering butterflies
flutter across the sky.

Here is a blue butterfly...
a purple butterfly...
a red butterfly...
and a green butterfly.

Butterflies can be just one color
or lots of different colors.

A hungry bird flies over the meadow.
The butterflies hide.
Can you find six butterflies here?

Butterflies love to land on flowers.
They sip the nectar.
It's their breakfast!

Dark clouds roll in.
They cover the sky.

It starts to rain.
Where does a butterfly go in the rain?

Maybe under a leaf.

The rain stops.
There is one rainbow in the sky
and another rainbow
of colorful butterflies!

One butterfly lands
on the very tip
of a blade of grass.

Butterflies are so light,
the blade of grass
does not even bend!

Soon the day is over.
Where do butterflies go at night?

Some rest in the tall grass.

The next morning,
the butterflies come out.
They warm their wings in the sun.
Then they fly off, looking for flowers
to land on today.

Maybe if you're lucky,
a butterfly will land on YOU!